Christmas TO Color

Color

Mary Tanana

HARPER

An Imprint of HarperCollinsPublishers

This book is dedicated to those who never close their minds
to new opportunities and creative paths.

Christmas to Color
By Mary Tanana
Copyright © 2015 by HarperCollins Publishers
All rights reserved. Printed in the United States of America.
No part of this book may be used or reproduced in any manner whatsoever without written
permission except in the case of brief quotations embodied in critical articles and reviews.
For information address HarperCollins Children's Books,
a division of HarperCollins Publishers, 195 Broadway, New York, NY 10007.
www.harpercollinschildrens.com

ISBN 978-0-06-244379-3

The artist used a Cintiq Wacom tablet to create the digital illustrations for this book.
Typography by Whitney Manger
Hand lettering by Valerie McKeehan
16 17 18 19   PC/WOR   10 9 8 7 6 5
❖
First Edition

This book belongs to

_____

Welcome to my winter wonderland!
In these pages, you'll find my visions of snowflakes
and stockings, reindeer and wreaths. I chose images and
symbols from celebrations around the world, as well as scenes from
my own imagination, to share the magic of Christmas with you.
Use gel pens, felt-tip pens, or colored pencils to add color, or use a black,
thin-tipped pen to add your own details and doodles. If you feel overwhelmed
at the sight of a box full of colored pencils, you can choose your four or five
favorite colors and start with them, or experiment with a series of different shades
of the same color. Remember, there's no wrong way to color these images:
each one will be a reflection of you and your personality!
Part of the wonder of Christmas is being able to make it your own: from
your grandmother's cookie recipe to the ornament you made as a
child hanging on your tree. My drawings are meant to help you
capture some of this Christmas magic, so sit back with
your favorite pens and start coloring!

Mary Tanana

My Influences

I'm fascinated by folk art traditions from all over the world. I'm really drawn to the folk art from the Ukraine, Hungary, Russia, and Poland, including the art of paper cutting. I also love the delicate henna designs from India. Whenever I travel, I take lots of photographs to remind me of the wealth of art and architecture that I've been blessed to experience.

I'm an avid gardener, and so my other big inspiration is Mother Nature! I'm captivated by the shapes, colors, and textures in flowers, shrubs, and trees. My love of nature also comes out in the organic, flowing shapes in my art.

Behind the Scenes:
How I Create My Art to Color

I start by drawing. I've learned that I think best with a pencil in my hand. Once I've drawn several objects that might go together on a page, I scan my sketches into an Adobe program on my computer. Then I play! I experiment with scale and where the objects are placed on the page. I do that until I'm satisfied with the composition. Then I add more fine-line work and create multiple layers to add intricacy to the designs. I use a Wacom Cintiq tablet to create my illustrations.

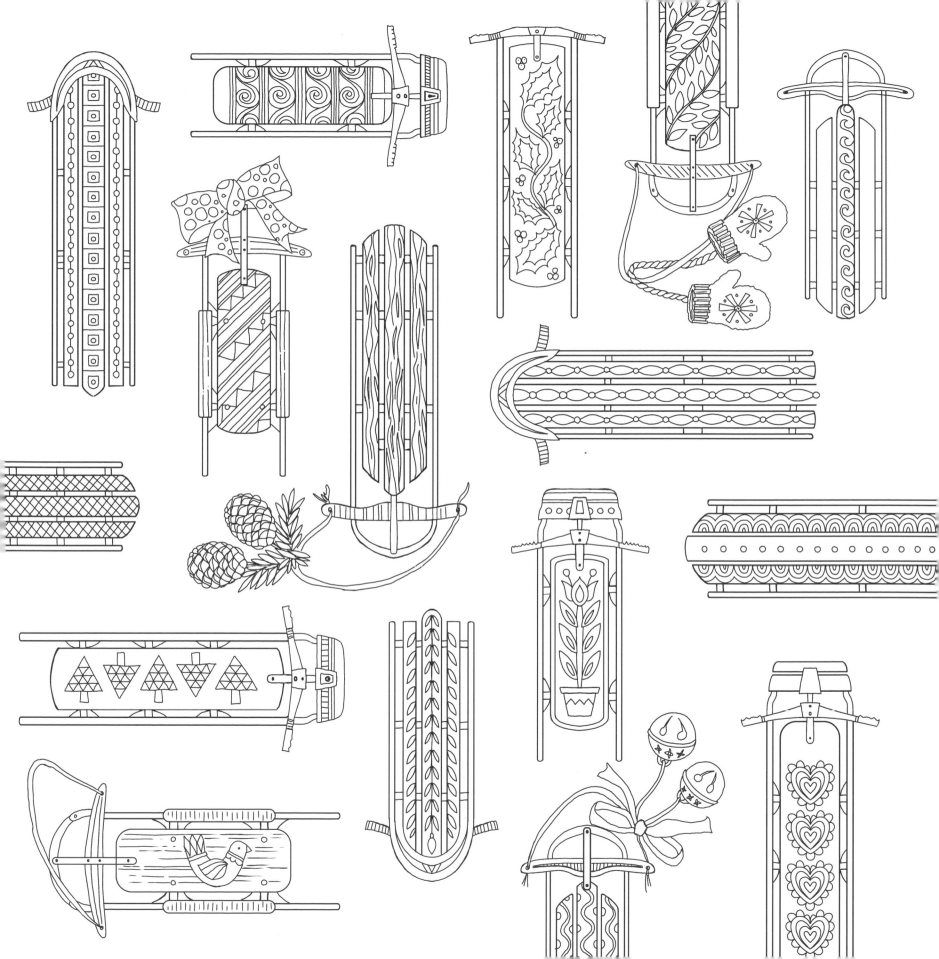

About the Author

I have loved doing crafts since I was six years old, especially embroidery, needlepoint, cross-stitch, quilting, and crochet! My parents were wonderful, encouraging me with each new interest. In college I studied fashion illustration, which led to my discovery of surface pattern design, and I completely fell in love with it! I left Syracuse University with a BFA in Fashion Illustration, and landed a job as a jewelry designer in a company that photo-etched gold and silver jewelry. My job was drawing intricate designs that were pierced and etched to create patterns in fine metals. Later I designed jewelry using gemstones, including diamonds. I traveled the world and was based in Hong Kong, where I led a large group of designers and frequently commuted into mainland China. My travels have had a huge influence on me—I have been so inspired by the rich cultures I've been exposed to.

When I came back to America, I rediscovered my earlier passion for surface design. I enrolled in many courses, including at Rhode Island School of Design, and have subsequently devoted my energies to the world of pattern!

I live in Rhode Island in a sunny seaside cottage, with my husband and some quirky kittens.

Mary Tanana